AF342365

KERI RUSSELL

A Real-Life Reader Biography

Judy Hasday

Mitchell Lane Publishers, Inc.
P.O. Box 619 • Bear, Delaware 19701

Copyright © 2001 by Mitchell Lane Publishers. All rights reserved. No part of this book may be reproduced without written permission from the publisher. Printed and bound in the United States of America.

First Printing

Real-Life Reader Biographies

Selena	Robert Rodriguez	Mariah Carey	Rafael Palmeiro
Tommy Nuñez	Trent Dimas	Cristina Saralegui	Andres Galarraga
Oscar De La Hoya	Gloria Estefan	Jimmy Smits	Mary Joe Fernandez
Cesar Chavez	Chuck Norris	Sinbad	Paula Abdul
Vanessa Williams	Celine Dion	Mia Hamm	Sammy Sosa
Brandy	Michelle Kwan	Rosie O'Donnell	Shania Twain
Garth Brooks	Jeff Gordon	Mark McGwire	Salma Hayek
Sheila E.	Hollywood Hogan	Ricky Martin	Britney Spears
Arnold Schwarzenegger	Jennifer Lopez	Kobe Bryant	Derek Jeter
Steve Jobs	Sandra Bullock	Julia Roberts	Robin Williams
Jennifer Love Hewitt	**Keri Russell**	Sarah Michelle Gellar	Liv Tyler
Melissa Joan Hart	Drew Barrymore	Alicia Silverstone	Katie Holmes
Winona Ryder	Alyssa Milano	Freddie Prinze, Jr.	Enrique Iglesias
Christina Aguilera			

Library of Congress Cataloging-in-Publication Data
Hasday, Judy L., 1957-
    Keri Russell / Judy Hasday.
        p. cm. — (A Real-life reader biography)
    Includes Index.
    ISBN 1-58415-033-5 (lib. bdg.)
    1. Russell, Keri, 1976- —Juvenile literature. 2. Actors—United States—Biography—Juvenile literature. [1. Russell, Keri, 1976- 2. Actors and actresses. 3. Women—Biography.] I. Title. II. Series.
PN2287.R825 H37 2001
791.45'028'092—dc21
[B]
00-042819

ABOUT THE AUTHOR: Judy L. Hasday, a native of Philadelphia, Pennsylvania, received her B.A. in communications and her Ed.M. in instructional technologies from Temple University. A multimedia professional, she has had her photographs published in many magazines and books. As a successful freelance author, Ms. Hasday has written several books, including an award-winning biography of James Earl Jones and biographies of Madeleine Albright and Tina Turner. She is the coauthor of *Marijuana,* a book for adolescents that presents the facts and dangers of using the drug. Recent works include a book about the Japanese attack on Pearl Harbor and the Apollo 13 mission.
PHOTO CREDITS: Cover: Globe Photos; p. 4 Globe Photos; p. 12 Victor Malafronte/Archive Photos; p. 18 Kobal Collection; p. 20 Corbis; p. 24 Lisa Rose/Globe Photos; p. 28, 29 Globe Photos
ACKNOWLEDGMENTS: The following story has been thoroughly researched, and to the best of our knowledge, represents a true story. While every possible effort has been made to ensure accuracy, the publisher will not assume liability for damages caused by inaccuracies in the data, and makes no warranty on the accuracy of the information contained herein. This story has not been authorized nor endorsed by Keri Russell.

Table of Contents

Chapter 1
Almost Too Pretty

In 1998, Keri Russell was at a crossroads in her career. She was looking for a special role that she could "sink her teeth into." Though she had been acting since she was fifteen, Keri felt most of the characters she had portrayed, in film and on television, were rather superficial. She thought of her first movie role. In 1992 she played the part of Mandy Park in *Honey, I Blew Up the Kid.* During an interview with *Detour* magazine, Keri said, "I was there to be the cute girl and kiss the guy. Literally that was my job. I can't tell you how many times I've been paid just to kiss the main guy."

Just when Keri was feeling discouraged, her agent—the person who acts as a representative between an actor and a studio looking for talent—sent her a script to read for a new television show called *Felicity.* Keri fell in love with the lead character, Felicity Porter. She asked her agent to get her an audition—a performance of the character in front of the show's creators. She realized that many people would come out to audition for the few parts available. This meant there would be a lot of competition, but, she wanted to try anyway.

The creators of *Felicity,* longtime friends J.J. Abrams and Matt Reeves, already thought they knew what Felicity Porter should look like when Keri came into the room to audition. In an article in *People* magazine in 1999, Abrams explains, "The character was always intended to be played by someone who was plain-looking. Keri is so gorgeous. She was too attractive to play Felicity, yet she couldn't have been more right. She is so natural, funny and engaging."

On the day of the audition, Keri sat and watched as many other girls ahead of her went in to see Abrams and Reeves. After waiting two hours, her name was finally called. Keri took a deep breath and promised herself to do her best. And she did, because Abrams and Reeves loved her performance, even though they thought Felicity should be a shy, average-looking girl. Keri's naturally curly long hair, emerald green eyes, wholesome appearance, and lively personality convinced both men that Keri was Felicity.

Keri Lynn Russell was born on March 23, 1976, to parents David and Stephanie Russell. They had originally planned to name their new daughter after her grandfather Kermit. However, Kermit didn't seem to be an appropriate name for a girl, so they shortened it to Keri. Keri is the second of three Russell children. Todd, Keri's brother, is four years older than she is, and her sister, Julie, is three years younger.

Keri is from Fountain Valley, a residential community in Orange

County. It is just a few miles from the beach and the Pacific Ocean.

Keri did not stay long in California. Her father was an executive for the Nissan Corporation. One day he came home and told the family that he was being transferred. First, the Russells moved to Dallas, Texas. Several years later, David Russell moved the family to Mesa, Arizona. Having only lived in Southern California, Keri was not used to the rugged, mountainous terrains of Texas and Arizona.

Shortly after the Russell family settled in the city of Mesa, Keri's sister was born. Keri was used to being the youngest, getting most of her parents' attention. But the new baby took up most of their time, and Keri had to spread her wings and make some friends. Her extracurricular activities included being a Brownie. However, when Keri and her best friend became a little too boisterous (loud), they were dropped from the Scout troop. Years later, during an appearance on *The Tonight Show with Jay Leno*, Keri laughed as she recalled the incident, saying their crime was something as silly as "doing too many cartwheels."

There were plenty of other things for Keri to do in Mesa, including playing softball and running track. By the time she reached the sixth grade, Keri was going through her "geeky stage." She wore braces on her teeth for two years and had "three tier high" mall bangs. While still a preteen, Keri discovered something new and exciting—the art of dance. She loved dancing, all kinds and styles: jazz, ballet, tap, and street dancing. Though she couldn't know it at the time, Keri's interest in dance would play an important role in her future.

Chapter 2
Chapter 2
Traveling Girl

Once Keri discovered dance, she thought she might make it her career. She spent almost all of her free time studying and practicing a variety of dance styles. Her mother was very supportive. She drove Keri from one dance class to another. Keri became a very good dancer. She earned scholarships at various dance studios. At one point she was taking seventeen classes a week! Between her schoolwork and dance classes, there was little time for anything else. Yet Keri didn't mind. She was very dedicated and worked hard. She was thrilled when she was

At one point Keri was taking seventeen dance classes a week.

selected to join the Mesa Stars Dance and Drill Team.

Keri met many new people and made new friends as a Mesa Star. Performing with them was exciting for the twelve-year-old. The Stars traveled around the country. They performed at major sporting events. They entertained the crowds at National Basketball Association games and performed for the fans at halftime at National Football League games. Keri even got to travel outside the United States. She went halfway around the world, to Sydney, Australia, in 1988. The Stars were invited to perform at the World's Fair Expo there. Traveling at such a young age taught Keri how to be independent. She didn't mind being away from home and her family.

Keri was also a good student. Despite her busy schedule, she kept up with her schoolwork. She maintained a high grade point average. She was a happy, well-adjusted teenager. She had friends and interests and was doing well in school. All of that changed when her father came home and told the family

Although Keri was born in California, her family moved many times when she was young.

they would be moving again. Nissan was transferring David to Denver, Colorado. Keri was devastated. How could she leave her friends? The Mesa Stars? Her dance scholarships? Her school? Moving meant many changes for Keri—a new school, new kids, new home—all of which could be overwhelming for a thirteen-year-old.

But Keri had plenty going for her. She had blossomed into quite an attractive young teen. Because of her dance training, she never really went through the awkward physical development stage that many teenagers do. She had a shapely figure from the endless hours of dance practice. Her emerald-green eyes sparkled when she smiled. Her curly golden brown hair cascaded down over her shoulders. Her hair was so beautiful that many of the other girls wanted to have their hair done to look just like Keri's.

Living in Denver was a new experience for Keri. The temperature outside was not as warm as it was in Fountain Valley or Mesa. In the winter months, Denver could get very cold. Keri's surroundings looked different, too. It snowed in Colorado. She had never seen snow before. But Denver was also very pretty. Keri could look out her window and see the picturesque Rocky Mountains adorning the sky in the distance.

Because Keri moved around so much, she had to learn how to adapt to her new surroundings. That included school and friends. During an interview on the TV show *Entertainment Tonight,* Keri explained how she felt: "I moved to Colorado at kind of a crucial time, just when I was finishing junior high school.

Because Keri moved around so much, she had to learn how to adapt to her new surroundings.

And that's a bad time to move. Because everyone kind of has their friends." Fortunately during an orientation for new students at Highlands Ranch High School, Keri met a girl who was also new in town. The two became fast friends. Because Keri was a stranger to most of her classmates, she didn't really fit in any group. Not fitting in gave her a chance to develop her own personality.

Keri did well in her new school. She picked up right where she left off in junior high school, getting straight As. Many of her high-school teachers remember Keri fondly. In an interview in the Denver *Rocky Mountain News*, teacher Beth Francis said of Keri, "She was one of those kids who stood out from the crowd. There are kids who do well and are dynamic that stand out in your mind. You'll never forget them. She was one of those kids."

Keri's magnetic personality and wholesome good looks also got the attention of a photographer in Denver. He believed that Keri had the looks and physical build to be a successful teen model. Ever the adventurous type, Keri decided to give it a try. She hated it. Her modeling career ended almost as quickly as it had begun. It was not as glamorous as many people think it is. Keri thought it was just plain boring. She didn't enjoy sitting for long periods of time and being "directed" as to how to sit, how to look at the camera, how to smile, and when not to smile. Keri preferred the kinds of activities that required her total concentration, like dance, so she resumed her dance studies. By now she had become quite good. It would be through her dancing that Keri would fall into her acting career.

Chapter 3
Life With Mickey

One night while Keri was practicing at the dance studio, two talent scouts were visiting.

One night while Keri was practicing at the dance studio, two talent scouts were visiting. These scouts were special—they worked for the Walt Disney Company. The Disney Studio began with Walt Disney's creation of a cartoon mouse named Mickey in 1928. Over the years the studio produced such animated movie classics as *Snow White and the Seven Dwarfs, Bambi,* and *Fantasia.* Today, the Disney empire also includes their famed theme parks: Disneyland in California, Disney World in Orlando, Florida, and others throughout the world; television networks; internet portals; and many other holdings.

With the invention of television, Walt Disney created several programs, including *The Mickey Mouse Club.* It was one of their most popular shows. Kids in the 1950s grew up watching the original Mouseketeers, such as Annette Funicello. Many other well-known stars also wore the famous Mickey Mouse ears. Past Mouseketeers include Lisa Whelchel from the famed TV show *Facts of Life,* Justin Timberlake and JC Chasez from the group 'N Sync, and teen singing sensation Britney Spears.

With the addition of cable TV, Disney launched its own network called the Disney Channel. Many of the family-oriented programs produced by Disney are carried on their cable channel. Disney scouts began looking for new, young faces for *The New Mickey Mouse Club.* The motion picture division was also casting for a new movie called *Honey, I Blew Up the Kid.*

Keri did very well at the auditions and got both parts. At fifteen, Keri

The motion picture division of the Walt Disney Company was casting for a new movie.

Keri in Honey, I Blew Up the Kid

Russell was going to be a Mouseketeer and act in her first movie.

Keri had never been to a professional audition before. A few years later, in an interview with *Seventeen,* Keri told writer Sarah Goldsmith that she never dreamed of being an actor.

Because *The New Mickey Mouse Club* was taped at the Disney World complex in Orlando, Florida, Keri had to move again. The rest of the Russell family moved to Florida, too. At home,

Keri was still treated like a regular kid. Her parents wanted to keep Keri grounded, not allowing her sudden star status to go to her head.

As a Mouseketeer, Keri began her growth as a performer. In time she became more comfortable in front of the camera. She developed the patience necessary to endure the long hours on the set for taping the show. She honed her social skills, learning to work as a team member with the crew and her castmates. She learned about the promotional side of the business, too. As a cast member, Keri gave interviews. She wrote a short biography to reveal a little bit of the private Keri to the public. It was on the show, however, where Keri got to display her talent as a singer and dancer.

Keri loved every minute of her three years—from 1991 to 1993—as a Mouseketeer. When asked about her time as a Mouseketeer, Keri says she had the best time of her life. In some ways she grew up in Disney World. She learned to drive in the Magic Kingdom and got to go on the rides in the theme parks for free. It was a pretty exciting time for the sixteen-year-old. *Honey, I Blew Up the Kid* was also filmed during her time in Florida. Keri felt that the self-discipline she learned from being a dancer helped her a lot with her acting. She told *TV Guide* that to her, "acting is really all choreography and timing."

While in the land of Mickey Mouse, Keri met fellow Mouseketeer Tony Lucca. She describes Tony as "hot and cute, and an amazing singer and musician." They became friends and then started dating. Keri often tells of how she kissed Tony for the first

time when she was fifteen. They worked together on the Mickey Mouse Club, but their personal relationship was on again, off again.

The show ended in 1993. Seventeen-year-old Keri wondered what she should do next. She thought about going to college. By then though, Keri loved acting and wanted to try to make it in Hollywood. Moving back to California meant leaving behind the comfort and security of family and friends again. But her experiences taught her that things have a way of working themselves out in life. She decided to go to California to pursue her dream.

Chapter 4
New Challenges

One of the first things Keri did when she moved back to California was sign with an agent. Then she started going to auditions for television commercials. That was easy for Keri. She had already spent hours in front of the television cameras as a Mouseketeer.

Keri's very first commercial was for Jack-In-The-Box restaurant. She also did work for Sears, JC Penney, and Lee Jeans. The acting was not very exciting, but Keri was earning good money. She was living on her own and had to learn to be self-reliant.

Keri began expanding her acting range. From commercials she moved on

Keri's very first commercial was for Jack-In-The-Box restaurant.

to television. She guest starred on some very popular prime-time shows. One of them was the teen hit *Boy Meets World.* As she has often described many of her early roles, this was one of those "just kiss the guy" parts.

Keri went from guest roles to costar in two short-lived TV series, *Emerald Cove* and *Daddy's Girls.* She especially enjoyed working on *Daddy's Girls.* "I was definitely the rookie, but I learned a lot working with people like Dudley Moore."

In early 1995 Keri won her first big role in *The Babysitter's Seduction.* The NBC movie was made especially for television. Keri costarred with veteran actors Felicia Rashad and Stephen Collins. She left quite an impression on her costars. In an article in *Seventeen,* Stephen Collins said of Keri, "It was so clear to me that she was someone who was going to be a star. At nineteen, she was already one of the most seasoned pros in the business."

In 1996 Aaron Spelling, the producer of such smash TV hits as *Dynasty, Beverly Hills 90210,* and *Melrose*

Keri thought her role on Malibu Shores *was very shallow.*

Place, was looking for hot, young talent to star in his new show *Malibu Shores.* Keri wouldn't have missed a chance to audition. She got the part of Chloe Walker, a rich kid who falls for a working-class guy. The first person Keri called with the good news was her mother. Screaming in the phone, Keri said, "Hi! I totally got the part."

Malibu Shores turned out to be all glitz and glamour. Keri was disappointed that the show was portraying women in such a superficial way. However, *Malibu Shores* did offer her the most visible role of her career.

Unfortunately the show was canceled after only eight episodes.

Despite the failure of *Malibu Shores,* Keri's career was going well. She got three acting jobs in a row. First she appeared in the independent film *Eight Days a Week.* Though the film was not widely released, it did receive critical praise.

In the spring of 1997 Keri finished work on *When Innocence Is Lost.* In her third project of the year, she appeared on the premiere episode of the Fox television show *Roar.* Unfortunately for Keri, her character, Claire, was killed off in the first episode.

Keri edged closer to stardom with her noteworthy performance in the film *The Curve.* In her role as Emma, Keri is part of a group of devious female college students who commit murder to further their own careers. The movie was shown at the Sundance Film Festival in Utah. The annual event features the best independent films of the year.

More and more people in the acting community were noticing Keri's

More and more people in the acting community were noticing Keri's work.

Keri wanted to play more challenging roles.

work. She was at the point in her career where she wanted to be cast in more challenging roles. Then she received the script for the show *Felicity*. When she finished reading it, she knew she had found that challenging role in the show's lead character, Felicity Porter.

Chapter 5
Now and the Future

Keri Russell often has a smile on her face. She has said, "I'm such a massive geek. I think I have huge, happy endorphins in my body." With such a successful career, she has good reason to be happy with her life.

She confesses that she "just fell into acting" and has "never left the party." The show *Felicity* is a hit. Keri loves the character she plays. In a recent interview in *Biography* magazine, Keri explained, "I admire her naive honesty—Felicity is free to say what's on her mind. I have a little censor in my brain that says, 'Don't do that.' But

With such a successful career, Keri has good reason to be happy with her life.

Keri with the cast of Felicity

Felicity doesn't. She does what she feels is right for her."

Keri wants to be a positive role model. She has often expressed that there is a lack of "real girls on TV" these days. She doesn't consider herself a glamour girl. Actually, she prefers being natural. She doesn't wear makeup. She is happiest wearing comfortable jeans and sweaters. Keri's character Felicity Porter is very much the same, and that's what Keri enjoys most about portraying her. "I love the fact that she doesn't wear makeup, has baggy clothes and has her hair in a ponytail," she said in an interview with *TV Guide.* "Most young girls out there look like her—not like the girls on *Baywatch.* I think it's a positive thing to see someone like her, who's smart and funny and can still be a basket case sometimes. She's human. They can finally see someone who's like them."

Keri's acting is also being applauded by her peers in the industry. In 1999 Keri won a Golden Globe for Best Performance by an Actress in a TV Series—Drama. She had stiff competition for the coveted award, including Roma Downey from *Touched by an Angel* and Julianna Margulies from *ER*.

After Keri auditioned for *Felicity*, she went to Ireland to shoot the film *Mad about Mambo*. In her lead role in the film, Keri teaches a soccer player how to dance to improve his game.

When she's not working, Keri relaxes at her home in Pacific Palisades, California,

Keri's love of acting earned her a Golden Globe Award in 1999.

with cat Nala and live-in love Tony. They reunited in 1998 and have been together since. Though not yet engaged, they wear matching silver bands. The rings are inscribed: "Neither you without me, nor me without you."

In her free time, Keri enjoys shopping. She also loves to take long walks or to in-line skate in her neighborhood. When her family is in town, no visit is complete without the traditional Russell backyard barbecue. Tony shares Keri's love of the outdoors. They enjoy hiking and camping trips.

What would Keri do if her television and film career were to end tomorrow? She'd move on to other projects. She loves to travel and has recently developed a passion for photography. Ultimately she'd like to travel around the world and take awesome pictures along the way. As she told *Biography* reporter Sheryl Altman, "The whole point of life is to experience a little bit of everything, and I think it's better when there are a few surprises thrown in."

Keri loves to travel and has recently developed a passion for photography.

Filmography

Felicity (1998-present)
Cinderelmo (1999)
Mad about Mambo (1999)
The Curve (1998)
Roar (1997)
When Innocence Is Lost (1997)
7th Heaven (guest appearance) (1997)
Eight Days a Week (1997)
The Lottery (1996)
Malibu Shores (1996)
The Babysitter's Seduction (1995)
Married…With Children (guest appearance) (1995)
Daddy's Girl (1994)
Emerald Cove (1994)
Always (Bon Jovi Music Video) (1994)
Boy Meets World (guest appearance) (1994)
The New Mickey Mouse Club (1991-1993)
Honey, I Blew Up the Kid (1992)

Chronology

- Born March 23, 1976, in Fountain Valley, California; mother: Stephanie; father: David
- Began studying dance while attending Keno Junior High School in Mesa, Arizona, and toured the country and elsewhere with the Mesa Stars Dance and Drill Team
- At age 13 family moved to Denver, Colorado
- At age 15 tried modeling, but hated it, preferring dance
- In 1991 joined the cast of *The All New Mickey Mouse Club* on the Disney Channel
- Cast in Walt Disney's feature film *Honey, I Blew Up the Kid* in 1992
- Moved to Los Angeles, California, in 1993 and began guest starring on TV shows, including *Boy Meets World* and *Married . . . With Children* before being cast as a regular with Dudley Moore in the TV sitcom *Daddy's Girls* in 1994
- Costarred in her first TV movie: NBC's *The Babysitter's Seduction,* 1995
- Joined the cast of TV producer Aaron Spelling's *Malibu Shores,* 1996
- Starred in feature film, *Eight Days a Week,* and two made-for-television movies, *When Innocence Is Lost* and *Roar,* in 1997
- After auditioning for the role of Felicity Porter for the new WB series *Felicity,* flew to Dublin, Ireland, to work on the film *Mad about Mambo* in 1998
- Signed contract for starring role in *Felicity;* debut: September 29, 1998
- Won Golden Globe for Best Actress in Drama series, 1999
- Played a princess in *Cinderelmo,* 1999
- *Felicity* returned to the WB lineup for its third season, 2000

Index